Is 2 a Lot?

Written by
Annie Watson

Illustrated by
Rebecca Evans

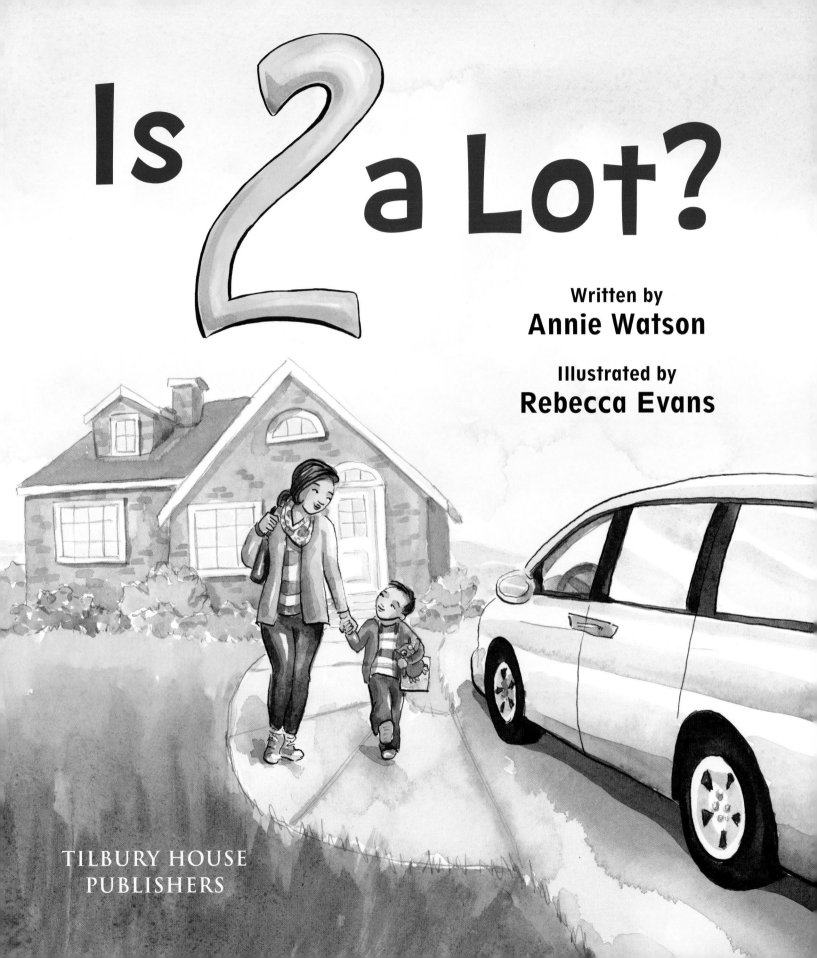

TILBURY HOUSE
PUBLISHERS

For Joey, Ben, and all children
who ask wonderful questions.
—AW

For my Joey, because I love that you
want to discover how everything works.
Never stop asking!
—RE

Tilbury House Publishers
12 Starr Street
Thomaston, Maine 04861
800-582-1899 · www.tilburyhouse.com

Text © 2019 by Annie Watson
Illustrations © 2019 by Rebecca Evans

Hardcover ISBN 978-0-88448-715-9
eBook ISBN 978-0-88448-717-3

First hardcover printing March 2019

15 16 17 18 19 20 XXX 10 9 8 7 6 5 4 3 2

Library of Congress Control Number: 2019931363

Designed by Frame25 Productions
Printed in Korea through Four Colour Print Group

One day Joey had a very important question.

"Is **2** a lot?" he asked his mommy.

His mommy thought for a moment. Then she said,

"Well, **TWO** is not a lot of pennies . . .

"but **TWO** is a lot of smelly skunks."

"What about 3?" Joey asked.

"Is 3 a lot?"

"Well, Joey," his mommy replied, "I'd say THREE is not a lot of books on a shelf . . .

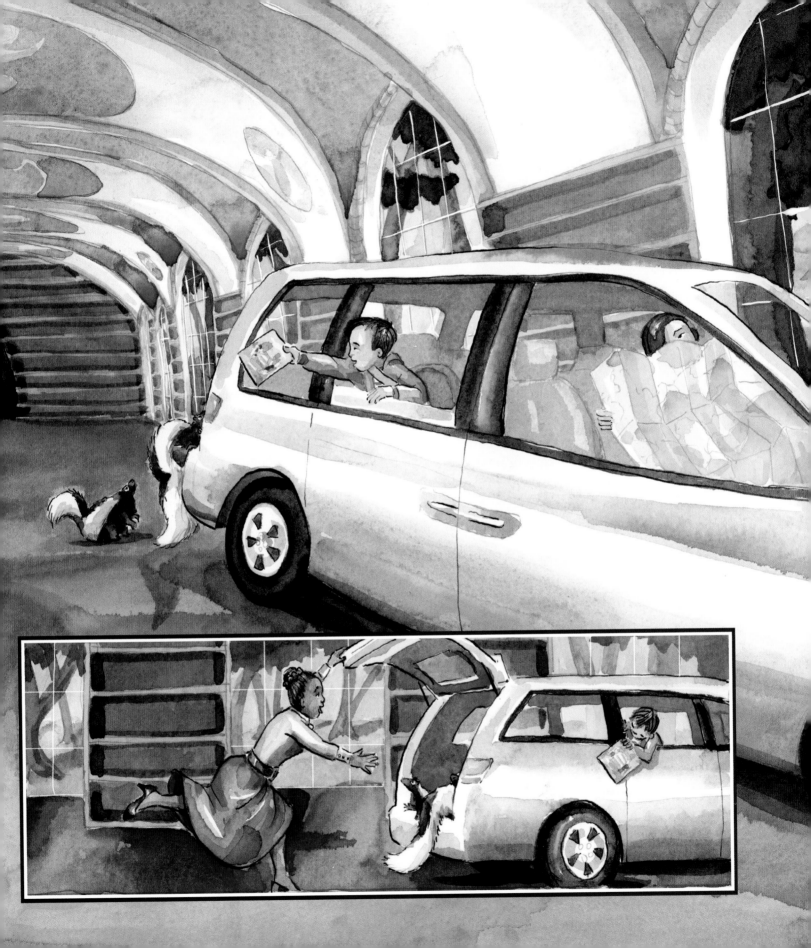

"but **THREE** is a lot of broken bones."

"What about 4?" asked Joey.

"Is 4 a lot?"

His mommy smiled.

"FOUR is not a lot of children in a school bus," she answered, "but it is a lot of dogs to walk at once."

"What about 5?" asked Joey.

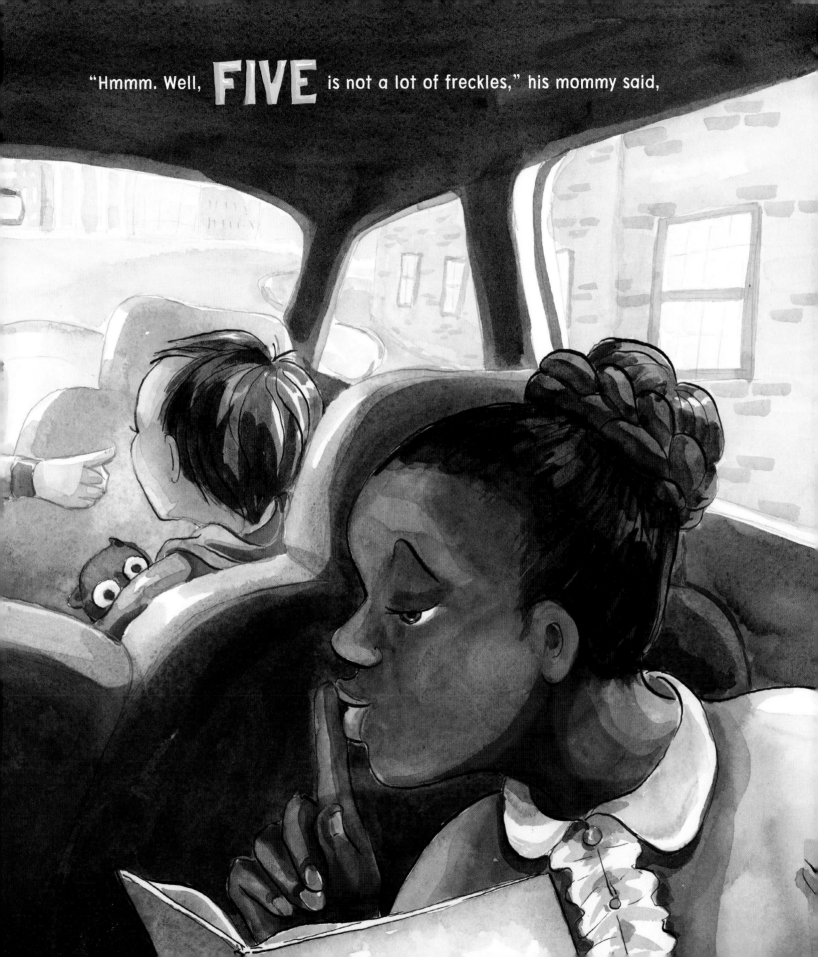

"Hmmm. Well, **FIVE** is not a lot of freckles," his mommy said,

"but FIVE is a lot of cowboys on a city street."

"What about 10, Mommy?"

"I had a feeling that was coming," said his mommy.

"I'd say TEN is not a lot of pieces of popcorn,

but it is a lot of chomping dinosaurs."

"What about 50 ?" asked Joey. "Is 50 a lot?"

"That's a hard one, Joey! Let me see . . . I'd say FIFTY is not a lot

of leaves left on an aspen tree, but it is a lot of letters in a mailbox."

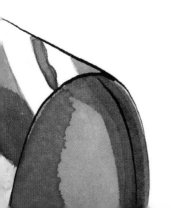

This time, Joey was sure he could stump his mommy.

"What about **100**?"

Mommy paused for a moment, and then she said,

" **ONE HUNDRED** is not a lot of snowflakes . . .

"but **ONE HUNDRED** is a lot of candles on a cake."

Joey took a deep breath and thought hard. Then he asked,

"Mommy, what about **1,000**? Is **1,000** a lot?"

Mommy said, "You ask such great questions!

I'd say **ONE THOUSAND** is not a lot of grains of sand . . .

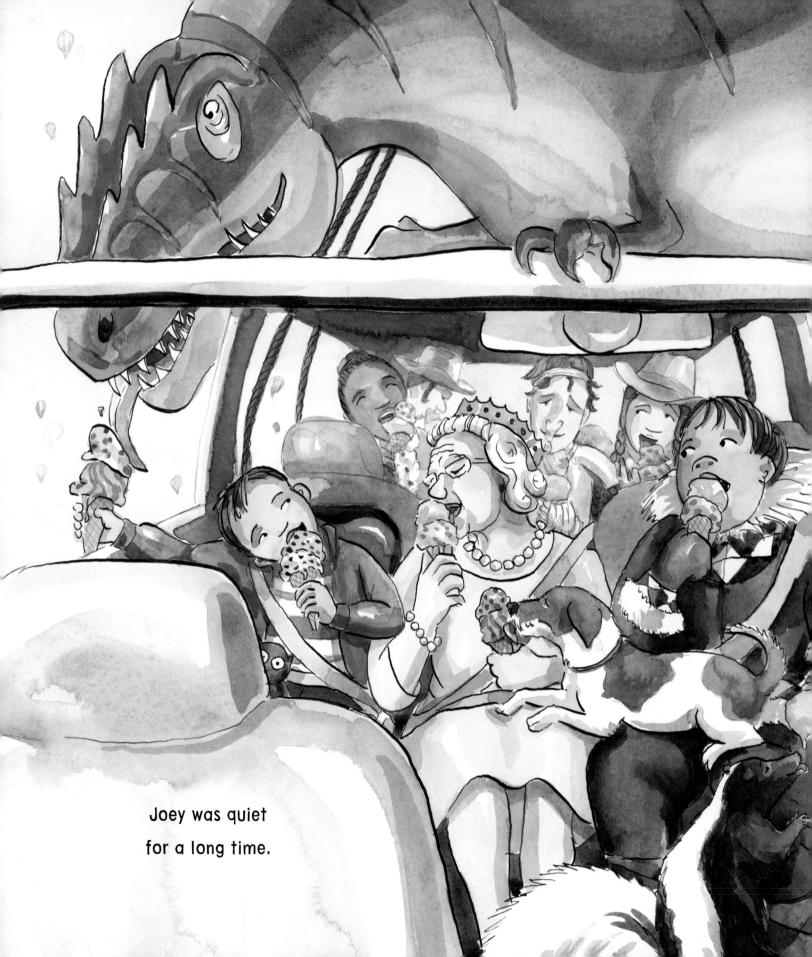

Joey was quiet
for a long time.

Then his mommy asked him, "So what do you think, Joey? Is **TWO** a lot?"

Joey answered, "Well, sometimes **2** is a lot . . .